PURITAN PASSIONS

BY

NATHANIEL HAWTHORNE

British Library Cataloguing-in-Publication Data
A catalogue record for this book is available from
the British Library

Contents

NATHANIEL HAWTHORNE

Nathaniel Hawthorne was born in Salem, Massachusetts, USA in 1804. Between 1821 and 1824, he attended Bowdoin College in Brunswick, Maine, along with fellow poet Henry Wadsworth Longfellow and future American President Franklin Pierce. A shy, bookish youth, Hawthorne was writing from a young age, and published his first novel, *Fanshawe,* in 1828. Over the next ten years, he attempted to become a professional writer, supplementing his earnings with a job as a Boston Custom House measurer. In 1842, he married Sophia Peabody and moved to The Manse in Concord, the epicentre of the burgeoning Transcendentalist movement.

Hawthorne's collection of short stories *Mosses from an Old Manse* was published in 1846, and four years later, he published his labour of love, the novel *The Scarlet Letter*. An immediate success, the novel remains widely read to this day, and allowed Hawthorne to devote himself full-time to his writing. Over the rest of his life, he produced six more novels, and a large amount of short stories. Aside from *The Scarlet Letter*, his best-known novel is probably *The Marble Faun*, and his best-remembered short stories include 'My Kinsman', 'Major Molineux', 'Young Goodman Browne' and 'Feathertop'.

Hawthorne died in 1864, following a long period of illness which included bouts of dementia. Though Hawthorne himself was perpetually dissatisfied with his body of work, he remains lauded as one of the greatest American writers, and *The Scarlet Letter* remains a standard school text in the USA. In 1879, Henry James called Hawthorne "the most valuable example of the American genius."

PURITAN PASSIONS

NATHANIEL HAWTHORNE

✳

"DICKON," cried Mother Rigby, "a coal for my pipe!"

The pipe was in the old dame's mouth when she said these words. She had thrust it there after filling it with tobacco, but without stooping to light it at the hearth, where indeed there was no appearance of a fire having been kindled that morning. Forthwith, however, as soon as the order was given, there was an intense red glow out of the bowl of the pipe, and a whiff of smoke from Mother Rigby's lips. Whence the coal came, and how brought thither by an invisible hand, I have never been able to discover.

"Good!" quoth Mother Rigby, with a nod of her head. "Thank ye, Dickon! And now for making this scarecrow. Be within call, Dickon, in case I need you again."

The good woman had risen thus early (for as yet it was scarcely sunrise) in order to set about making a scarecrow which she intended

3

to put in the middle of her corn-patch. It was now the latter week of May, and the crows and blackbirds had already discovered the little green, rolled-up leaf of the Indian corn just peeping out of the soil. She was determined, therefore, to contrive as life-like a scarecrow as ever was seen, and to finish it immediately from top to toe, so that it should begin its sentinel's duty that very morning. Now Mother Rigby (as everybody must have heard) was one of the most cunning and potent witches in New England, and might, with very little trouble, have made a scarecrow ugly enough to frighten the minister himself. But on this occasion, as she had awakened in an uncommonly pleasant humour, and was further dulcified by her pipe of tobacco, she resolved to produce something fine, beautiful, and splendid, rather than hideous and horrible.

"I don't want to set up a hobgoblin in my own corn-patch, and almost at my own doorstep," said Mother Rigby to herself, puffing out a whiff of smoke; "I could do it if I pleased, but I'm tired of doing marvellous things, and so I'll keep within the bounds of everyday business, just for variety's sake. Besides, there is no use in scaring the little children for a mile roundabout, though 'tis true I'm a witch."

It was settled therefore in her own mind, that the scarecrow should represent a fine gentleman of the period, so far as the materials at hand would allow. Perhaps it may be as well to enumerate the chief of the articles that went to the composition of this figure.

The most important item of all, probably, although it made so little show, was a certain broomstick, on which Mother Rigby had taken many an airy gallop at midnight, and which now served the scarecrow by way of a spinal column, or, as the unlearned phrase it, a backbone. One of its arms was a disabled flail which used to be wielded by Goodman Rigby, before his spouse worried him out of this troublesome world; the other, if I mistake not, was composed of the pudding stick and a broken rung of a chair, tied loosely together at the elbow. As for its legs, the right one was a hoe-handle, and the left an undistinguished and miscellaneous stick from the woodpile. Its lungs, stomach, and other affairs of that kind were nothing better than a meal-bag stuffed with straw. Thus we have made out the skeleton and entire corporeity of the scarecrow, with the exception of its head; and this was admirably supplied by a somewhat withered and shrivelled pumpkin, in which Mother Rigby cut two holes for the eyes, and a slit for the mouth, leaving a bluish-coloured knob in the middle to pass for a nose. It was really quite a respectable face.

"I've seen worse ones on human shoulders, at any rate," said

Mother Rigby. "And many a fine gentleman has a pumpkin-head, as well as my scarecrow."

But the clothes in this case were to be the making of the man. So the good old woman took down from a peg an ancient plum-coloured coat of London make and with relics of embroidery on its seams, cuffs, pocket-flaps, and buttonholes, but lamentably worn and faded, patched at the elbows, tattered at the skirts, and thread-bare all over. On the left breast was a round hole, whence either a star of nobility had been rent away, or else the hot heart of some former wearer had scorched it through and through. The neighbours said that this rich garment belonged to the Black Man's wardrobe, and that he kept it at Mother Rigby's cottage for the convenience of slipping it on whenever he wished to make a grand appearance at the governor's table.

To match the coat there was a velvet waistcoat of very ample size and formerly embroidered with foliage that had been as brightly golden as the maple-leaves in October, but which had now quite van-ished out of the substance of the velvet. Next came a pair of scarlet breeches once worn by the French governor of Louisbourg, and the knees of which had touched the lower step of the throne of Louis le Grand. The Frenchman had given these smallclothes to an Indian pow-wow, who parted with them to the old witch for a gill of strong waters, at one of their dances in the forest. Furthermore, Mother Rigby produced a pair of silk stockings and put them on the figure's legs, where they showed as unsubstantial as a dream with the wooden reality of the two sticks making itself miserably apparent through the holes. Lastly, she put her dead husband's wig on the bare scalp of the pumpkin, and surmounted the whole with a dusty three-cornered hat, in which was stuck the longest tail-feather of a rooster.

Then the old dame stood the figure up in a corner of her cottage and chuckled to behold its yellow semblance of a visage, with its nobby little nose thrust into the air. It had a strangely self-satisfied aspect, and seemed to say, "Come look at me!"

"And you are well worth looking at, that's a fact!" quoth Mother Rigby, in admiration at her own handiwork. "I've made many a puppet since I've been a witch; but methinks this is the finest of them all. 'Tis almost too good for a scarecrow. And, by the by, I'll just fill a fresh pipe of tobacco, and then take him out to the corn-patch."

While filling her pipe, the old woman continued to gaze with almost motherly affection at the figure in the corner. To say the truth, whether it were chance, or skill, or downright witchcraft, there was something wonderfully human in this ridiculous shape, bedizened with its tattered finery; and as for the countenance, it appeared to shrivel its yellow surface into a grin—a funny kind of expression betwixt scorn and merriment—as if it understood itself to be a jest at mankind. The more Mother Rigby looked the better she was pleased.

"Dickon," cried she, sharply, "another coal for my pipe!"

Hardly had she spoken, when, just as before, there was a red-glowing coal on the top of the tobacco. She drew in a long whiff and puffed it forth again into the bar of morning sunshine which struggled through the one dusty pane of her cottage window. Mother Rigby always liked to flavour her pipe with a coal of fire from the particular chimney-corner whence this had been brought. But where the chimney-corner might be, or who brought the coal from it—further than that invisible messenger seemed to respond to the name of Dickon—I cannot tell.

"That puppet yonder," thought Mother Rigby, still with her eyes fixed on the scarecrow, "is too good a piece of work to stand all summer in a corn-patch, frightening away the crows and black-birds. He's capable of better things. Why, I've danced with a worse one, when partners happened to be scarce, at our witch-meetings in the forest! What if I should let him take his chance among the other men of straw and empty fellows who go bustling about the world?"

The old witch took three or four more whiffs at her pipe and smiled.

"He'll meet plenty of his brethren at every street-corner!" continued she. "Well, I didn't mean to dabble in witchcraft today, further than the lighting of my pipe; but a witch I am, and a witch I'm likely to be, and there's no use in trying to shirk it. I'll make a man of my scarecrow, were it only for the joke's sake!"

While muttering these words, Mother Rigby took the pipe from her own mouth and thrust it into the crevice which represented the same feature in the pumpkin visage of the scarecrow.

"Puff, darling, puff!" said she. "Puff away, my fine fellow! Your life depends on it!"

This was a strange exhortation, undoubtedly, to be addressed to a mere thing of sticks, straw, and old clothes, with nothing better than a shrivelled pumpkin for a head; as we know to have been the scarecrow's case. Nevertheless, as we must carefully hold in remembrance, Mother Rigby was a witch of singular power and dexterity; and keeping this fact duly before our minds, we shall see nothing beyond credibility in the remarkable incidents of our story. Indeed, the great difficulty will be at once got over if we can only bring ourselves to believe that as soon as the old dame bade him puff, there came a whiff of smoke from the scarecrow's mouth. It was the very feeblest of whiffs, to be sure; but it was followed by another and another, each more decided than the preceding one.

"Puff away, my pet; puff away, my pretty one!" Mother Rigby kept repeating, with her pleasant smile. "It is the breath of life to ye; and that you may take my word for."

Beyond all question the pipe was bewitched. There must have been a spell either in the tobacco or in the fiercely glowing coal that so mysteriously burned on top of it, or in the pungently aromatic smoke which exhaled from the kindled weed. The figure, after a few doubtful attempts, at length blew forth a volley of smoke extending all the way from the obscure corner into the bar of sunshine. There it eddied and melted away among the motes of dust. It seemed a convulsive effort; for the two or three next whiffs were fainter, although the coal still glowed and threw a gleam over the scarecrow's visage. The old witch clapped her skinny hands together, and smiled encouragingly upon her handiwork. She saw that the charm worked well. The shrivelled, yellow face, which heretofore had been no face at all, had already a thin, fantastic haze, as it were, of human likeness, shifting to and fro across it; sometimes vanishing entirely, but growing more perceptible than ever with the next whiff from the pipe. The whole figure, in like manner, assumed a show of life. If we must needs pry closely into the matter, it may be doubted whether there was any real change, after all, in the sordid, worn-out, worthless and ill-jointed substance of the scarecrow; but merely a spectral illusion, and a cunning effect of light and shade so coloured and contrived as to delude the eyes of most men. The miracles of witchcraft seem always to have had a very shallow subtlety; and, at least, if the above explanation do not hit the truth of the process, I can suggest no better.

"Well puffed, my pretty lad!" still cried old Mother Rigby. "Come, another good stout whiff, and let it be with might and main. Puff for thy life, I tell thee! Puff out of the very bottom of thy heart; if any heart thou hast, or any bottom to it! Well done, again! Thou didst suck in that mouthful as if for the pure love of it."

And then the witch beckoned to the scarecrow, throwing so much magnetic potency into her gesture that it seemed as if it must inevitably be obeyed.

"Why lurkest thou in the corner, lazy one?" said she. "Step forth! Thou hast the world before thee!"

In obedience to Mother Rigby's word, and extending its arms as if to reach her outstretched hand, the figure made a step forward— a kind of hitch and jerk, however, rather than a step—then tottered and almost lost its balance. What could the witch expect? It was nothing after all, but a scarecrow stuck upon two sticks. But the strong-willed old beldam scowled and beckoned, and flung the energy of her purpose so forcibly at this poor combination of rotten wood and musty straw and ragged garments, that it was compelled to show itself a man, in spite of the reality of things.

So it stepped into the bar of sunshine. There it stood—poor devil of a contrivance that it was!—with only the thinnest vesture of human similitude about it, through which was evident the stiff, rickety, incongruous, faded, tattered, good-for-nothing patchwork of its substance, ready to sink in a heap on the floor, as conscious of its own unworthiness to be erect. Shall I confess the truth? At its present point of vivification, the scarecrow reminds me of some of the lukewarm and abortive characters, composed of heterogeneous materials, used for the thousandth time, and never worth using, with which romance writers (and myself, no doubt, among the rest) have so overpeopled the world of fiction.

But the fierce old hag began to get angry and show a glimpse of her diabolic nature (like a snake's head peeping with a hiss out of her bosom) at this pusillanimous behaviour of the thing which she had taken the trouble to put together.

"Puff away, wretch!" cried she, wrathfully. "Puff, puff, puff, thou thing of straw and emptiness! thou rag or two! thou meal-bag! thou pumpkin-head! thou nothing! Where shall I find a name vile enough to call thee by? Puff, I say, and suck in thy fantastic life along with the smoke; else I snatch the pipe from thy mouth and hurl thee where that red coal came from."

Thus threatened, the unhappy scarecrow had nothing for it but to puff away for dear life. As need was, therefore, it applied itself lustily to the pipe and sent forth such abundant volleys of tobacco smoke that the small cottage-kitchen became all vaporous. The one sunbeam struggled mistily through, and could but imperfectly define the image of the cracked and dusty window-pane on the opposite wall. Mother Rigby, meanwhile, with one brown arm akimbo and the other stretched towards the figure, loomed grimly amid the obscurity with such port and expression as when she was wont to heave a ponderous nightmare on her victims and stand at the bedside to enjoy their agony. In fear and trembling did this poor scarecrow puff. But its efforts, it must be acknowledged, served an excellent purpose; for, with each successive whiff, the figure lost more and more of its dizzy and perplexing tenuity and seemed to take denser substance. Its very garments, moreover, partook of the magical change, and shone with the gloss of novelty and glistened with the skilfully embroidered gold that had long been rent away. And, half revealed among a smoke, a yellow visage bent its lustreless eyes on Mother Rigby.

At last the old witch clenched her fist and shook it at the figure. Not that she was positively angry, but merely acting on the principle —perhaps untrue, or not the only truth, though as high a one as Mother Rigby could be expected to attain—that feeble and torpid natures, being incapable of better inspiration, must be stirred up by fear. But here was the crisis. Should she fail in what she now sought to effect, it was her ruthless purpose to scatter the miserable simulacrum into its original elements.

"Thou hast a man's aspect," said she, sternly. "Have also the echo and mockery of a voice! I bid thee speak!"

The scarecrow gasped, struggled, and at length emitted a murmur, which was so incorporated with its smoky breath that you could scarcely tell whether it were indeed a voice or only a whiff of tobacco. Some narrators of this legend held the opinion that Mother Rigby's conjurations, and the fierceness of her will, had compelled a familiar spirit into the figure, and that the voice was his.

"Mother," mumbled the poor stifled voice, "be not so awful with me! I would fain speak; but being without wits, what can I say?"

"Thou canst speak, darling, canst thou?" cried Mother Rigby, relaxing her grim countenance into a smile. "And what shalt thou say, quotha! Say, indeed! Art thou of the brotherhood of the empty skull, and demandest of me what thou shalt say? Thou shalt say a thousand things, and saying them a thousand times over, thou shalt still have said nothing! Be not afraid, I tell thee! When thou comest into the world (whither I purpose sending thee forth-with), thou shalt not lack the wherewithal to talk. Talk! Why, thou shalt babble like a mill-stream, if thou wilt. Thou hast brains enough for that, I trow!"

"At your service, mother," responded the figure.

"And that was well said, my pretty one," answered Mother Rigby. "Then thou spakest like thyself, and meant nothing. Thou shalt have a hundred such set phrases, and five hundred to the boot of them. And now, darling, I have taken so much pains with thee, and thou art so beautiful, that, by my troth, I love thee better than any witch's puppet in the world; and I've made them of all sorts—clay, wax, straw, sticks, night-fog, morning-mist, sea-foam, and chimney-smoke. But thou art the very best. So give heed to what I say."

"Yes, kind mother," said the figure, "with all my heart!"

"With all thy heart!" cried the old witch, setting her hands to her sides and laughing loudly. "Thou hast such a pretty way of speaking. With all thy heart! And thou didst put thy hand to the left side of thy waistcoat, as if thou really hadst one!"

So now, in high good humour with this fantastic contrivance of hers, Mother Rigby told the scarecrow that it must go and play its part in the great world, where not one man in a hundred, she affirmed, was gifted with more real substance than itself. And, that he might hold up his head with the best of them, she endowed him, on the spot, with an unreckonable amount of wealth. It consisted partly of a gold mine in Eldorado, and of ten thousand shares in a broken bubble, and of half a million acres of vineyard at the North Pole, and of a castle in the air, and a château in Spain, together with all the rents and income therefrom accruing. She further made over to him the cargo of a certain ship, laden with salt of Cadiz, which she herself, by her necromantic arts, had caused to founder, ten years before, in the deepest part of mid-ocean. If the salt were not dissolved, and could be brought to market, it would fetch a pretty penny among the fishermen. That he might not lack ready money, she gave him a copper farthing of Birmingham manufacture, being all the coin she had about her, and likewise a great deal of brass, which she applied to his forehead, thus making it yellower than ever.

"With that brass alone," quoth Mother Rigby, "thou canst pay thy way all over the earth. Kiss me, pretty darling! I have done my best for thee."

Furthermore, that the adventurer might lack no possible advantage towards a fair start in life, this excellent old dame gave him a token by which he was to introduce himself to a certain magistrate, member of the council, merchant, and elder of the church (the four capacities constituting but one man), who stood at the head of society in the neighbouring metropolis. The token was neither more nor less than a single word which Mother Rigby whispered to the scarecrow, and which the scarecrow was to whisper to the merchant.

"Gouty as the old fellow is, he'll run thy errands for thee, when once thou hast given him that word in his ear," said the old witch. "Mother Rigby knows the worshipful Justice Gookin, and the worshipful Justice knows Mother Rigby!"

Here the witch thrust her wrinkled face close to the puppet's, chuckling irrepressibly, and fidgeting all through her system, with delight at the idea which she meant to communicate.

"The worshipful Master Gookin," whispered she, "hath a comely maiden to his daughter. And hark ye, my pet! Thou hast a fair outside, and a pretty wit enough of thine own. Yea, a pretty wit enough! Thou wilt think better of it when thou hast seen more of other people's wits. Now, with thy outside and thy inside, thou art the very man to win a young girl's heart. Never doubt it! I tell thee it shall be so. Put but a bold face on the matter, sigh, smile, flourish thy hat, thrust forth thy leg like a dancing-master, put thy right hand to the left side of thy waistcoat, and pretty Polly Gookin is thine own!"

All this while the new creature had been sucking in and exhaling the vapoury fragrance of his pipe, and seemed now to continue the occupation as much for the enjoyment it afforded as because it was an essential condition of his existence. It was wonderful to see how exceedingly like a human being it behaved. Its eyes (for it appeared to possess a pair) were bent on Mother Rigby, and at suitable junctures it nodded or shook its head. Neither did it lack words proper for the occasion: "Really! Indeed! Pray tell me! Is it possible! Upon my word! By no means! Oh! Ah! Hem!" and other such weighty utterances as imply attention, inquiry, acquiescence, or dissent on the part of the auditor. Even had you stood by and seen the scarecrow made, you could scarcely have resisted the conviction that it perfectly understood the cunning counsels which the old witch poured into its counterfeit of an ear. The more earnestly it applied its lips to the pipe the more distinctly was its human likeness stamped among visible realities, the more sagacious grew its expression, the more life-like its gestures and movements, and the more intelligibly audible its voice. Its garments, too, glistened so much the brighter with an illusionary magnificence. The very pipe, in which burned the spell of all this wonder-work, ceased to appear as a smoke-blackened earthen stump, and became a meerschaum, with painted bowl and amber mouthpiece.

It might be apprehended, however, that as the life of the illusion seemed identical with the vapour of the pipe, it would terminate simultaneously with the reduction of the tobacco to ashes. But the beldam foresaw the difficulty.

"Hold thou the pipe, my precious one," said she, "while I fill it for thee again."

It was sorrowful to behold how the fine gentleman began to fade back into a scarecrow while Mother Rigby shook the ashes out of the pipe and proceeded to replenish it from her tobacco-box.

"Dickon," cried she, in her high, sharp tone, "another coal for this pipe!"

No sooner said than the intensely red speck of fire was glowing within the pipe bowl; and the scarecrow, without waiting for the witch's bidding, applied the tube to his lips and drew in a few short, convulsive whiffs, which soon, however, became regular and equable.

"Now, mine own heart's darling," quoth Mother Rigby, "whatever may happen to thee, thou must stick to thy pipe. Thy life is in it; and that, at least, thou knowest well, if thou knowest nought besides. Stick to thy pipe, I say! Smoke, puff, blow thy cloud; and tell the people, if any question be made, that it is for thy health, and that so the physician orders thee to do. And, sweet one, when thou shalt find thy pipe getting low, go apart into some corner and (first filling thyself with smoke) cry sharply, 'Dickon, a fresh pipe of tobacco!' and 'Dickon, another coal for my pipe!' and have it into thy pretty mouth as speedily as may be. Else, instead of a gallant gentleman in a gold-laced coat, thou wilt be but a jumble of sticks and tattered clothes, and a bag of straw, and a withered pumpkin! Now depart, my treasure, and good luck go with thee!"

"Never fear, mother!" said the figure, in a stout voice, and sending forth a courageous whiff of smoke. "I will thrive, if an honest man and a gentleman may!"

"Oh, thou wilt be the death of me!" cried the old witch, convulsed with laughter. "That was well said. If an honest man and a gentleman may! Thou playest thy part to perfection. Get along with thee for a smart fellow; and I will wager on thy head, as a man of pith and substance, with a brain, and what they call a heart, and all else that a man should have, against any other thing on two legs. I hold myself a better witch than yesterday, for thy sake. Did not I make thee? And I defy any witch in New England to make such another! Here; take my staff along with thee!"

The staff, though it was but a plain oaken stick, immediately took the aspect of a gold-headed cane.

"That gold head has as much sense in it as thine own," said Mother Rigby, "and it will guide thee straight to worshipful Master Gookin's door. Get thee gone, my treasure; and if any ask thy name, it is Feathertop. For thou hast a feather in thy hat, and I have thrust a handful of feathers into the hollow of thy head, and thy wig, too, is of the fashion they call Feathertop—so be Feathertop thy name!"

And, issuing from the cottage, Feathertop strode manfully towards town. Mother Rigby stood at the threshold, well pleased to see how the sunbeams glistened on him, as if all his magnificence were real, and how diligently and lovingly he smoked his pipe, and how handsomely he walked, in spite of a little stiffness of his legs. She watched him until out of sight, and threw a witch benediction after her darling, when a turn of the road snatched him from her view.

Betimes in the forenoon, when the principal street of the neighbouring town was just at its acme of life and bustle, a stranger of very distinguished figure was seen on the sidewalk. His port as well as his garments betokened nothing short of nobility. He wore a richly embroidered plum-coloured coat, a waistcoat of costly velvet magnificently adorned with golden foliage, a pair of splendid scarlet breeches, and the finest and glossiest of white silk stockings. His head was covered with a peruke, so daintily powdered and adjusted that it would have been sacrilege to disorder it with a hat; which therefore (and it was a gold-laced hat, set off with a snowy feather) he carried beneath his arm. On the breast of his coat glistened a star. He managed his gold-headed cane with an airy grace peculiar to the fine gentlemen of the period; and, to give the highest possible finish to his equipment, he had lace ruffles at his wrist, of a most ethereal delicacy, sufficiently avouching how idle and aristocratic must be the hands which they half concealed.

It was a remarkable point in the accoutrement of this brilliant personage, that he held in his left hand a fantastic kind of a pipe, with an exquisitely painted bowl and an amber mouthpiece. This he applied to his lips as often as every five or six paces, and inhaled a deep whiff of smoke, which, after being retained a moment in his lungs, might be seen to eddy gracefully from his mouth and nostrils.

As may well be supposed, the street was all astir to find out the stranger's name.

"It is some great nobleman, beyond question," said one of the townspeople. "Do you see the star at his breast?"

"Nay; it is too bright to be seen," said another. "Yes; he must needs be a nobleman, as you say. But by what conveyance, think you, can his lordship have voyaged or travelled hither? There has been no vessel from the old country for a month past; and if he have arrived overland from the southward, pray where are his attendants and equipage?"

"He needs no equipage to set off his rank," remarked a third. "If he came among us in rags, nobility would shine through a hole in his elbow. I never saw such dignity of aspect. He has the old Norman blood in his veins, I warrant him."

"I rather take him to be a Dutchman, or one of your high Germans," said another citizen. "The men of those countries have always the pipe at their mouths."

"And so has a Turk," answered his companion. "But, in my judgment, this stranger hath been bred at the French court, and hath there learned politeness and grace of manner, which none understand so well as the nobility of France. That's gait, now! A vulgar spectator might deem it stiff—he might call it a hitch and jerk, but, to my eyes, it hath an unspeakable majesty, and must have been acquired by constant observation of the deportment of the Grand Monarque. The stranger's character and office are evident enough. He is a French ambassador, come to treat with our rulers about the cession of Canada."

"More probably a Spaniard," said another, "and hence his yellow complexion; or, most likely, he is from the Havana, or from some port on the Spanish main, and comes to make investigation about the piracies which our governor is thought to connive at. Those settlers in Peru and Mexico have skins as yellow as the gold which they dig out of their mines."

"Yellow or not," cried a lady, "he is a beautiful man"—so tall, sc slender! such a fine, noble face, with so well-shaped a nose, and al' that delicacy of expression about the mouth! And, bless me, how bright his star is! It positively shoots out flames!"

"So do your eyes, fair lady," said the stranger, with a bow and a flourish of his pipe; for he was just passing at the instant. "Upon my honour, they have quite dazzled me."

"Was ever so original and exquisite a compliment?" murmured the lady, in an ecstasy of delight.

Amid the general admiration excited by the stranger's appearance, there were only two dissenting voices. One was that of an impertinent cur, which after snuffing at the heels of the glittering figure, put its tail between its legs and skulked into its master's back yard, vociferating an execrable howl. The other dissentient was a young child, who squalled at the fullest stretch of his lungs, and babbled some unintelligible nonsense about a pumpkin.

Feathertop, meanwhile, pursued his way along the street. Except for the few complimentary words to the lady, and now and then a slight inclination of the head in requital of the profound reverences of the bystanders, he seemed wholly absorbed in his pipe. There needed no other proof of his rank and consequence than the perfect equanimity with which he comported himself, while the curiosity and admiration of the town swelled almost into clamour around him. With a crowd gathering behind his footsteps, he finally reached the mansion-house of the worshipful Justice Gookin, entered the gate, ascended the steps of the front door, and knocked. In the interim, before his summons was answered, the stranger was observed to shake the ashes out of his pipe.

"What did he say in that sharp voice?" inquired one of the spectators.

"Nay, I know not," answered his friend. "But the sun dazzles my eyes strangely. How dim and faded his lordship looks all of a sudden! Bless my wits, what is the matter with me?"

"The wonder is," said the other, "that his pipe, which was out only an instant ago, should be all alight again, and with the reddest coal I ever saw. There is something mysterious about this stranger. What a whiff of smoke was that! Dim and faded did you call him? Why, as he turns about, the star on his breast is all ablaze."

"It is, indeed," said his companions; "and it will go near to dazzle pretty Polly Gookin, whom I see peeping at it out of the chamber-window."

The door being now opened, Feathertop turned to the crowd, made a stately bend of his body like a great man acknowledging the reverence of the meaner sort, and vanished into the house. There was a mysterious kind of a smile, if it might not better be called a grin or grimace, upon his visage; but of all the throng that beheld him not an individual appears to have possessed insight enough to detect the illusive character of the stranger except a little child and a cur dog.

Our legend here loses somewhat of its continuity, and, passing over the preliminary explanations between Feathertop and the merchant, goes in quest of the pretty Polly Gookin. She was a damsel of a soft, round figure, with light hair and blue eyes, and a fair, rosy face, which seemed neither very shrewd nor very simple. This young lady had caught a glimpse of the glistening stranger while standing at the threshold, and had forthwith put on a laced cap, a string of beads, her finest kerchief, and her stiffest damask petticoat, in preparation for the interview. Hurrying from her chamber to the parlour, she had ever since been viewing herself in the large looking-glass and practising pretty airs—now a smile, now a ceremonious dignity of aspect, and now a softer smile than the former, kissing her hand likewise, tossing her head, and managing her fan; while within the mirror an unsubstantial little maid repeated every gesture and did all the foolish things that Polly did, but without making her ashamed of them. In short, it was the fault of pretty Polly's ability rather than her will if she failed to be as complete an artifice as the illustrious Feathertop himself; and, when she thus tampered with her own simplicity, the witch's phantom might well hope to win her.

No sooner did Polly hear her father's gouty footsteps approaching the parlour door, accompanied with the stiff clatter of Feathertop's high-heeled shoes, than she seated herself bolt-upright and innocently began warbling a song.

"Polly! daughter Polly!" cried the old merchant. "Come hither, child."

Master Gookin's aspect, as he opened the door, was doubtful and troubled.

"This gentleman," continued he, presenting the stranger, "is the

Chevalier Feathertop—nay, I beg his pardon, my Lord Feathertop —who hath brought me a token of remembrance from an ancient friend of mine. Pay your duty to his lordship, child, and honour him as his quality deserves."

After these few words of introduction, the worshipful magistrate immediately quitted the room. But, even in that brief moment, had the fair Polly glanced aside at her father instead of devoting herself wholly to the brilliant guest, she might have taken warning of some mischief nigh at hand. The old man was nervous, fidgety, and very pale. Purposing a smile of courtesy, he had deformed his face with a sort of galvanic grin, which, when Feathertop's back was turned, he exchanged for a scowl, at the same time shaking his fist and stamping his gouty foot—an incivility which brought his retribution along with it.

The truth appears to have been, that Mother Rigby's word of introduction, whatever it might be, had operated far more on the rich merchant's fears than on his good-will. Moreover, being a man of wonderfully acute observation, he had noticed that the painted figures on the bowl of Feathertop's pipe were in motion. Looking more closely, he became convinced that these figures were a party of little demons, each duly provided with horns and a tail, and dancing hand in hand, with gestures of diabolical merriment, round the circumference of the pipe-bowl. As if to confirm his suspicions, while Master Gookin ushered his guest along a dusky passage from his private room to the parlour, the star on Feathertop's breast had scintillated actual flames, and threw a flickering gleam upon the wall, the ceiling, and the floor.

With such sinister prognostics manifesting themselves on all hands, it is not to be marvelled at that the merchant should have felt that he was committing his daughter to a very questionable acquaintance. He cursed, in his secret soul, the insinuating elegance of Feathertop's manners, as this brilliant personage bowed, smiled, put his hand on his heart, inhaled a long whiff from his pipe, and enriched the atmosphere with the smoky vapour of a fragrant and visible sigh. Gladly would poor Master Gookin have thrust his dangerous guest into the street; but there was a constraint and terror within him. This respectable old gentleman, we fear, at an earlier period of life, had given some pledge or other to the evil principle, and perhaps was now to redeem it by the sacrifice of his daughter.

It so happened that the parlour door was partly of glass, shaded by a silken curtain, the folds of which hung a little awry. So strong was the merchant's interest in witnessing what was to ensue between the fair Polly and the gallant Feathertop, that after quitting the room he could by no means refrain from peeping through the crevice of the curtain.

But there was nothing very miraculous to be seen; nothing—except the trifles previously noticed—to confirm the idea of a supernatural peril environing the pretty Polly. The stranger, it is true, was evidently a thorough and practised man of the world, systematic and self-possessed, and therefore the sort of a person to whom a parent ought not to confide a simple young girl, without due watchfulness for the result.

The worthy magistrate, who had been conversant with all degrees and qualities of mankind, could not but perceive every motion and gesture of the distinguished Feathertop came in its proper place; nothing had been left rude or native in him; a well-digested conventionalism had incorporated itself thoroughly with his substance and transformed him into a work of art. Perhaps it was this peculiarity that invested him with a species of ghastliness and awe. It is the effect of anything completely and consummately artificial, in human shape, that the person impresses us as an unreality and as having hardly pith enough to cast a shadow upon the floor. As regarded Feathertop, all this resulted in a wild, extravagant, and fantastical impression, as if his life and being were akin to the smoke that curled upward from his pipe.

But pretty Polly Gookin felt not thus. The pair were now promenading the room; Feathertop with his dainty stride and no less dainty grimace; the girl with a native maidenly grace, just touched, not spoiled, by a slightly affected manner, which seemed caught from the perfect artifice of her companion. The longer the interview continued, the more charmed was pretty Polly, until, within the first quarter of an hour (as the old magistrate noted by his watch), she was evidently beginning to be in love. Nor need it have been witchcraft that subdued her in such a hurry; the poor child's heart, it may be, was so very fervent that it melted her with its own warmth as reflected from the hollow semblance of a lover. No matter what Feathertop said, his words found depth and reverberation in her ear; no matter what he did, his action was heroic to her eye. And by this time it is to be supposed there was a blush on Polly's cheek, a tender smile about her mouth, and a liquid softness in her glance; while the star kept coruscating on Featurertop's breast, and the little demons careered with more frantic merriment than ever about the circumference of his pipe-bowl. O pretty Polly Gookin, why should these imps rejoice so madly that a silly maiden's heart was about to be given to a shadow! Is it so unusual a misfortune, so rare a triumph?

By and by Feathertop paused, and throwing himself into an imposing attitude, seemed to summon the fair girl to survey his figure and resist him longer if she could. His star, his embroidery, his buckles, glowed at that instant with unutterable splendour; the picturesque hues of his attire took a richer depth of colouring; there was a gleam and polish over his whole presence betokening the perfect witchery of well-ordered manners. The maiden raised her eyes and suffered them to linger upon her companion with a bashful and admiring gaze. Then, as if desirous of judging what value her own simple comeliness might have side by side with so much brilliancy, she cast a glance towards the full-length looking-glass in front of which they happened to be standing. It was one of the truest plates in the world, and incapable of flattery. No sooner did the images therein reflected meet Polly's eye than she shrieked, shrank from the stranger's side, gazed at him for a moment in the wildest dismay, and sank insensible upon the floor. Feathertop likewise had looked towards the mirror, and there beheld, not the glittering mockery of his outside show, but a picture of the sordid patchwork of his real composition, stripped of all witchcraft.

The wretched simulacrum! We almost pity him. He threw up his arms with an expression of despair that went further than any of his previous manifestations towards vindicating his claims to be reckoned human : for perchance the only time since this so often empty and deceptive life of mortals began its course, an illusion had seen and fully recognized itself.

Mother Rigby was seated by her kitchen hearth in the twilight of this eventful day, and had just shaken the ashes out of a new pipe, when she heard a hurried tramp along the road. Yet it did not seem so much the tramp of human footsteps as the clatter of sticks or the rattling of dry bones.

"Ha!" thought the old witch, "what step is that? Whose skeleton is out of its grave now, I wonder?"

A figure burst headlong into the cottage door. It was Feathertop!

His pipe was still alight; the star still flamed upon his breast; the embroidery still glowed upon his garments; nor had he lost, in any degree or manner that could be estimated, the aspect that assimilated him with our mortal brotherhood. But yet, in some indescribable way (as is the case with all that has deluded us when once found out), the poor reality was felt beneath the cunning artifice.

"What has gone wrong?" demanded the witch. "Did yonder sniffling hypocrite thrust my darling from his door? The villain! I'll set twenty fiends to torment him till he offer thee his daughter on his bended knees!"

"No, mother," said Feathertop, despondingly; "it was not that."

"Did the girl scorn my precious one?" asked Mother Rigby, her fierce eyes glowing like two coals of Tophet. "I'll cover her face with pimples! Her nose shall be as red as the coal in thy pipe! Her front teeth shall drop out! In a week hence she shall not be worth thy having!"

"Let her alone, mother," answered poor Feathertop; "the girl was half won; and methinks a kiss from her sweet lips might have made me altogether human. But," he added, after a brief pause and then a howl of self-contempt, "I've seen myself, mother! I've seen myself for the wretched, ragged, empty thing I am! I'll exist no longer!"

Snatching the pipe from his mouth, he flung it with all his might against the chimney, and at the same instant sank upon the floor a medley of straw and tattered garments, with some sticks protruding from the heap and a shrivelled pumpkin in the midst. The eyeholes were now lustreless; but the rudely carved gap, that just before had been a mouth, still seemed to twist itself into a despairing grin, and was so far human.

"Poor fellow!" quoth Mother Rigby, with a rueful glance at the relics of her ill-fated contrivance. "My poor, dear, pretty Feathertop! There are thousands upon thousands of coxcombs and charlatans in the world, made up of just such a jumble of worn-out, forgotten and good-for-nothing trash as he was! Yet they live in fair repute, and never see themselves for what they are. And why should my poor puppet be the only one to know himself and perish for it?"

While thus muttering, the witch had filled a fresh pipe of tobacco, and held the stem between her fingers, as doubtful whether to thrust it into her own mouth or Feathertop's.

"Poor Feathertop!" she continued. "I could easily give him another chance and send him forth again tomorrow. But no; his

20

feelings are too tender, his sensibilities too deep. He seems to have too much heart to bustle for his own advantage in such an empty and heartless world. Well! well! I'll make a scarecrow of him after all. 'Tis an innocent and à useful vocation, and will suit my darling well; and if each of his human brethren had as fit a one, 'twould be the better for mankind; and as for this pipe of tobacco, I need it more than he."

So saying Mother Rigby put the stem between her lips. "Dickon!" cried she, in her high, sharp tone, "another coal for my pipe!"